dedicated to
NATALIE

First published in Great Britain in 1997
by Ragged Bears Limited,
Ragged Appleshaw,
Andover,
Hampshire SP11 9HX

A CIP record of this book is available from the British Library

ISBN 1 85714 121 0

Printed in Hong Kong

Nila's Little Green Book of Nursery Rhymes

By NILA AYE

RAGGED BEARS

a slice

Pat-a-cake, pat-a-cake,
baker's man,

Bake me a cake as fast as you can.

Pat it and prick it, and mark it with **B**,

And put it in the **oven** for baby and me.

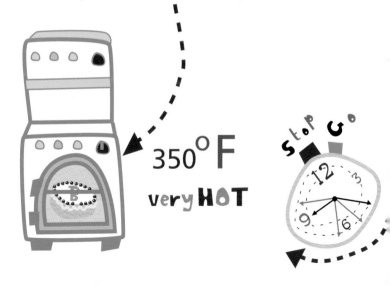

350°F

very**HOT**

stop Go

DING, DONG, BELL

Pussy's in the well.
Who put her in?
Little Johnny Green.
Who pulled her out?
Little Tommy Stout.

What a naughty boy was that,
To try to drown poor pussy-cat,
Who never did him harm,
And killed all the mice in his father's barn.

Hector Protector

was dressed all in green;
Hector Protector was sent to the Queen.
The Queen did not like him,
No more did the King;
So Hector Protector was sent back again.

Rover

Old Farmer Giles

Walked seven miles
With his faithful dog, old **Rover!**
And old Farmer Giles,
When he came to the stiles,
Took a run and jumped clean over.

Farmer Giles

over

stile

greenhouse

cockle shell

PRETTY MAIDS

MARY, MARY, quite contrary,
How does your garden grow?
With silver bells and cockle shells
And pretty maids all in a row.

Pease pudding hot,

Pease pudding cold,
Pease pudding in the pot,
Nine days old.

HOT　　　COLD　　　9 DAYS OLD

Some like it hot,
Some like it cold,
Some like it in the pot,
Nine days old.

HOT COLD 9 DAYS OLD

Doctor Foster went to Gloucester

In a shower of rain.
He stepped in a puddle
Right up to his middle
And never went there again.

puddle

Gloucester

his middle

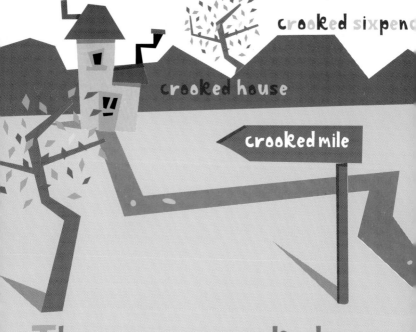

crooked sixpence

crooked house

crooked mile

There was a crooked man, a

He found a crooked sixpence against a crooked stile;
He bought a crooked cat, which caught a crooked mouse,
And they all lived together in a little crooked house.

6P

crooked stile

crooked man

crooked cat

crooked mouse

nd he walked a crooked mile,

Jack and Jill went up the hill
To fetch a pail of water.

Jack fell down and broke his crown,
And Jill came tumbling after.

Three blind mice, see how they run!
They all ran after the farmer's wife,
Who cut off their tails with a carving knife,
Did you ever see such a thing in your life,
As three blind mice?

The old woman must sta

nd at the tub, tub, tub,

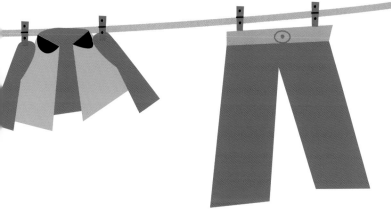

ashing powder

The dirty clothes to rub, rub, rub;
But when they are clean and fit to be seen,
She'll dress like a lady and dance on the green.

Space clock

8:00 p.m.

The Man in the Moon looked out of the moon,
And this is what he said:
" 'Tis time that now I'm getting up,
All children are in bed."